A catalogue record for this book is available from the British Library

Published by Ladybird Books Ltd
80 Strand, London, WC2R 0RL
A Penguin Company

002
© LADYBIRD BOOKS LTD MMVIII
This edition MMXIII

LADYBIRD and the device of a Ladybird are trademarks of Ladybird Books Ltd

ISBN: 978-0-71819-539-7

Printed in China

Ladybird
Stories for 4 year olds

Written by Joan Stimson
Illustrated by Debora Van de Leijgraff

Ernest takes a ride

Ernest Elephant had an
ambition. He wanted to ride
on a red bus. Each day Ernest
looked out from his enclosure. The buses went
by exactly on the hour. "The three o'clock bus
is the bus for me," thought Ernest. "Everyone will
be taking a nap after lunch." Then he made his plan.

One morning Mr Wainwright found a new notice in Ernest's enclosure.

Throw cash, not buns.
Am saving up.

Signed
Ernest Elephant

Mr Wainright was shocked – but the visitors loved it. In just one day Ernest became rich.

That night Ernest went to bed early, but he was too excited to sleep.

"Tomorrow," he kept thinking, "I shall ride on a red bus."

The next day, Ernest was too nervous to eat his breakfast. He was too jittery to eat his lunch. He was beginning to think that three o'clock would never come.

By five minutes to three, Mr Wainwright and the animals were snoring.

Heave! By two minutes to three Ernest had clambered onto the boundary wall of the zoo.

It was a real struggle, but Ernest made it.

At exactly three o'clock, the red bus arrived. Ernest dangled his trunk over the wall, right by the bus stop.

Eeek! The bus driver screeched to a halt. Ernest's trunk was blocking the road!

The bus had an open top, which lined up perfectly with the zoo wall, and Ernest stepped very gently on board. Then he settled comfortably into six seats.

The bus driver had got over his surprise, and he was beginning to feel quite important. He was looking forward to telling the other drivers he'd picked up an elephant!

11

But the bus conductor was beginning to feel nervous. What if the elephant didn't have the bus fare? He needn't have worried. Ernest had plenty of money. He handed it over with a note:

Return trip to the zoo – keep the change.
Signed
Ernest Elephant

The red bus drove through the country and into town. Ernest saw all the sights – the shops, the churches, the parks and the factories. He'd done it at last!

"I'm riding on a red bus, I'm riding on a red bus," hummed Ernest happily. Every few minutes the bus stopped. An old lady got on with her dog. A young boy got off with his hamster.

But there were no zebras, monkeys, seals or hippos at the bus stops. There was no sight of Mr Wainwright's friendly face. Ernest began to feel homesick – homesick and hungry.

At exactly four o'clock the red bus pulled up outside the zoo. Ernest got up from his six seats, and stepped gently back onto the zoo wall.

Thud! Ernest was back in his enclosure.

Mr Wainwright and the animals had stopped snoring. They were beginning to stir.

"It's great to be home," thought Ernest, and he nuzzled his trunk into Mr Wainwright's ear. Then he gave Mr Wainwright a playful push.

Mr Wainwright didn't need a note to know what Ernest wanted. Mr Wainwright could read Ernest like a book.

Ernest wanted his tea!

The jumble sale

Russell woke up and wriggled. He had tied a knot in his middle to remind himself of something.

"Snakes alive!" he cried. "It's the day of the jumble sale!"

Russell rummaged in his room. Before long, his rucksack was full and his shelves were empty.

Then Russell shook his moneybox. "I won't want to buy anything," he said. "Not now my room's so tidy."
But he took some money along – just in case.

The church hall was packed.

"Thank you, Russell," beamed the vicar's wife. She arranged Russell's things on a stall. Russell slithered up a table leg to get a better view.

Russell didn't enjoy seeing his things being sold.

"Special offer!" cried one of the helpers suddenly.

Russell rushed over to look. "Ooh, I haven't read these," he cried, reaching for some adventure stories.

"What about Snakes and Ladders?" asked another helper.

"Yes, please!" said Russell. Before long, his rucksack was full and he'd spent all his money.

Russell slid slowly home. He arranged his new collection of books and toys.

Russell yawned and wriggled into bed, then he looked across at his shelves. "There's no point in having shelves with nothing on them," he said.

And, of course, Russell was right.

Noisy Norman

Mrs Tortoise said that little tortoises should be seen and not heard. But you couldn't help hearing Norman! Norman was so noisy. Whenever he wanted to say anything, he yelled and shrieked. Whenever he went anywhere, he crashed and banged.

"I do wish Norman didn't get up so early," said Mrs Tortoise. "It's such a long day with all that noise."

Mr Tortoise had a bright idea. "Let's get Norman a paper round. Paper boys start at the crack of dawn."

Norman liked his new job. But he didn't just deliver the papers. He rattled the letterboxes and yelled, "Read all about it! Read all about it!" at the top of his voice.

Nobody wanted to read all about it – not at six o'clock in the morning. Norman got the sack.

"I do wish Norman didn't go to bed so late," said Mrs Tortoise. "It's such a long day with all that noise."

Mr Tortoise had another idea. "Norman can join a band. Musicians are meant to be noisy. And they work late."

The band leader gave Norman a triangle. He explained what to do, "Wait for the pianist to finish playing. Then go *ting, ting, ting.*"

But Norman couldn't wait for the pianist to finish. As soon as the music started, he went *CRASH, BANG, WALLOP!* He jumped up and down and shrieked out of tune.

The pianist was annoyed. The band leader was unhappy. He asked Norman to leave the band.

Mr Tortoise had run out of ideas, so Mrs Tortoise took Norman to the doctor.

The doctor jumped when Norman crashed into his surgery. He covered his ears when Norman yelled, "Hello!"

"I need some whisper medicine for Norman," said Mrs Tortoise.

The doctor looked through his catalogue. "I'm sorry," he said. "Whisper medicine hasn't been invented yet." He wrote something on a piece of paper and gave it to Mrs Tortoise.

It turned out to be the name of a karate school. Mrs Tortoise fixed up karate lessons straight away.

"Now you can jump up and down and be noisy," she told Norman.

"Just watch the others," said the instructor. "You can join in next week."

But Norman couldn't wait for next week. "Look at meeeee!" he shrieked. His cry shattered the windows in the karate hall.

The instructor was shattered, too, and he sent Norman home with a note.

Don't ever send Norman again!

Mrs Tortoise didn't know what to do next.
Then the fair came to town.

"Off you go," said Mrs Tortoise. "You can be as noisy
as you like at the fair."

Norman jumped up and down with excitement.
He was even noisier than usual.

"I want to go on
the dodgems,"
yelled Norman.
And suddenly
the dodgems
were full.

"I've won a coconut!"
shrieked Norman. And
suddenly everyone
was at the coconut shy.

"Lovely candy floss,"
cried Norman.
There was soon
a huge queue
for the candy floss.

The fairground manager came to see Norman's parents. "We don't need to advertise with Norman about," he said. "Can you spare him for a few evenings?"

What a wonderful arrangement!

Norman's big voice brought big business to the fair. And Mr and Mrs Tortoise had a rest – from Norman's noise!